Looking for Leprechauns

by ABBY KLEIN   illustrated by JOHN McKINLEY

SCHOLASTIC INC.

New York   Toronto   London   Auckland   Sydney
Mexico City   New Delhi   Hong Kong   Buenos Aires

To all those who believe in leprechauns…
never stop believing—A.K.

To Buff, with love—J.M.

ISBN-13: 978-0-545-09930-1
ISBN-10: 0-545-09930-7

12 11   14/0

Printed in the U.S.A.
First printing, February 2009

It was St. Patrick's Day, and I was excited!

I jumped out of bed, and I put on my green shark shirt.

Then I ran downstairs.

"Good morning," said my mom.

"Good morning," I said.

"You look very happy today, Freddy."

"I am very happy. Today is St. Patrick's Day. It's my lucky day!"

I sat down at the table, and I pinched my sister, Suzie.

"OUCH!" she yelled. "Why did you do that?"

"Freddy," said Mom, "don't pinch your sister."

"It's St. Patrick's Day," I told Suzie.

"So?" she said.

"You have to wear green on St. Patrick's Day."

"I don't have any green on," Suzie said.

"I know," I said. "That's why I pinched you."

Suzie stuck her tongue out at me.

"Freddy, tell your sister that you are sorry," said Mom.

"Sorry," I said. "But if you don't put green on, you'll get pinched at school."

At school, all of my friends wore something green.

Robbie wore dark green pants.

Jessie had on a green shirt just like me.

Max the bully had on a green hat.

Only Chloe didn't wear anything green.

So Max pinched her.

"Ow, ow, ow!" she cried.

Our teacher, Mrs. Wushy, came over.

"Chloe, why are you crying?"

"Max pinched me."

"She's not wearing anything green," Max said.

"It's not okay to pinch people," Mrs. Wushy said.

"But on St. Patrick's Day," Max said, "if you don't wear green, you get pinched."

"But I don't like green," said Chloe.
"My favorite color is pink."

"Here, put this on," said Mrs. Wushy.
She gave Chloe a green clover sticker.

Chloe put the sticker on her dress.

"You can't pinch me now," she said.

"I have green on."

Max walked away.

"Time for a story," our teacher said.
"This story is about a leprechaun."

"Leprechauns are from Ireland,"
said Robbie. "It's good luck to catch them."

Mrs. Wushy read the story.
It was about a man who tried
to catch a leprechaun.

He wanted the leprechaun's gold
at the end of the rainbow.
  But he couldn't catch him.
  The leprechaun was too fast and smart.

"I can catch a leprechaun," said Chloe.

"You cannot," said Max.

"Yes, I can."

"No, you can't."

"Stop fighting, you two," said Mrs. Wushy. "Now we are going to make some leprechaun pictures."

"Cool," I said. "I love leprechauns."

"Me, too," said Jessie.

Mrs. Wushy gave us each a paper.

It had the pieces of a leprechaun drawn on it.

I cut out all of the leprechaun pieces and glued them together.

"There," I said. "All done."

"That's cute," said Jessie.

"What's his name?"

"Larry," I said.

"That's a funny name," Jessie said.

I giggled. "Larry the Leprechaun."
I made Larry dance on the table.
"Look at me! I am Larry the dancing
leprechaun. You can't catch me."

Max tried to grab Larry, but he missed.
"Ha, ha, you can't catch me!" I said.

It was time to go outside for recess.

"I am going to look for leprechauns,"
I said.

"Me, too," said Robbie.

"Wait for me," said Jessie.

"Let's look under the slide," said Robbie.
"Do you see a leprechaun?"

"No," we said.

"Let's look in the grass," said Jessie.
"Good idea," I said.
We looked all over the grass.
No leprechauns.

"I know," said Robbie. "The leprechaun must
be hiding in the sand."

We ran to the sandbox and started to dig.

We dug and dug and dug, but we didn't find
a leprechaun.

"I don't know where else to look,"
said Jessie.

"Me, neither," said Robbie.

I hit my forehead with the palm of my hand.

"Think, think, think," I said to myself.
"If I were a leprechaun, where would I hide?"
Mrs. Wushy called us to line up.
"Oh, no!" we moaned.

"I don't think leprechauns are real,"
I said to my teacher.

"Why not, Freddy?" she asked.

"Well, we looked and looked, but we
couldn't find one."

"I'm sorry," said Mrs. Wushy, "but it's
time to go in now."

When we walked into the room, I couldn't believe my eyes.

There was a little gold nugget on each chair.

I ran over and picked one up.

"It's leprechaun gold!" I yelled. "It *is* my lucky day!"

"Mrs. Wushy, where did it come from?"
I asked.

"A leprechaun must have left it. Look, he also left this note. It says, 'Happy St. Patrick's Day, everyone!'"

We shouted, "Happy St. Patrick's Day to you, too, Mr. Leprechaun!"